THE GREEN BUTTON

Doug Merlin

Oxygen House Books

To all of our dogs. Past, present and future

CONTENTS

PREFACE

The rules were simple: you walked up to the black box and chose which button to press. Either the red one or the blue one. The red one would mean you were going on a trip to visit a cake factory. The blue would mean you were going to the cup final.

But when it was his turn, Noah saw something unexpected.

There was a red and blue button, but also a third, green button.

Nobody else had seen a green button. Even his teacher could not see one when she turned the box around.

What did it mean? Was he imagining it? What would happen if he pressed it?

THE GREEN BUTTON

CHAPTER ONE

"Greeny"

Noah had been waiting in line for ten minutes. It was his turn next. He was so excited.

"Which button are you going to press," whispered Jamie.

"The blue one," Noah said.

"Really? You're going to miss the cup final! You're mad."

He had decided on the Blue Trip this year. The blue coach was going to a **real** gold mine. Red or Blue were the two choices everyone got, and there was a button for each. Most of his friends said they had pressed the Red button to get a ticket for the trip to the cup final, and now it was his turn.

"Noah, come forward, please," snapped Ms Prince.

Noah walked up to the box and peered inside. What he saw was very unexpected. There were three buttons. One red, one blue… and one green.

"Excuse me, Ms Prince," said Noah. "What's the green button for?"

Ms Prince turned the box around and looked inside. "What green button? I can't see a green button in here. Stop messing about and choose, please. Or it's a day with Mr Thompson for you!"

Puzzled, Noah looked back into the box. There definitely was a green button in there. But he wasn't going to risk missing the trip. No way. So he made his choice. He pressed the blue button. Gold mine it was!"

At breaktime Noah stood in the playground with his friends.

"Did you see the green button?" he

asked Jamie.

"What green button?, No." Jamie replied.

"Did YOU see it Jen?"

"No."

"Did YOU see it Amy?"

"No, you are just imagining it."

He kept asking all of his friends the same question, and after a while, they got annoyed with him. The other kids started making fun of him. He continued to ask, and that earned him the nickname "Greeny" which he had to live with forever more.

The school day came to an end, and eventually he gave up asking- maybe he HAD imagined the green button. He walked home and focussed his thoughts on "Noah's Sweet Inventions"

Noah's Sweet Inventions was one of the best food channels on YouTube. Well, that was Noah's mum's opinion, anyway. She didn't understand why her son only had twenty-five subscribers. His channel was much more interesting than that horrible unwrapping channel Elijah from Noah's school had. Elijah's channel, *Elijah Gets More Stuff*, had over eight thousand subscribers! Noah's mum thought this was mad. It was just videos of Elijah unwrapping expensive stuff his dad had bought him and showing off.

Noah didn't understand it either. He worked really hard on *Noah's Sweet Inventions*. He'd been into cooking and making sweets since he was six years old. He was eleven now. After five years of inventing sweets, he'd become pretty amazing at it. He had posted videos of all his greatest sweet inventions. One video showed how to make his Caramel Cushions. These sweets were soft caramel marshmallows that warmed up your whole body on a cold day. Another video showed how to make his Fizzing Fire-

Chews. These were chewy sweets made with so much popping candy that little fireworks would shoot out your nose. And then there was Noah's favourite video: his Tangerine Tongue Toffees. These would turn your tongue bright orange!

They really were the most remarkable sweets. Everybody who tasted them loved them. But still, he only had a handful of subscribers. Some of them were family, but most were just mean people from school who left nasty comments. He only had two real, genuine followers, and one strange one which he could not find out about- it said "dot-gov". He occasionally tried to google it, but always got the same message: *'Classified*-private information- no access"

Noah's dream was to become a world-famous YouTuber with his sweet inventions. Of course, it would be amazing to be famous. Being famous would mean Noah could share his inventions with the world. It would be wonderful to be respected for his sweet-making skills. But it would also mean he could help his little brother, Isaac.

Noah lived at home with Isaac and his mum. Isaac was seven and should have been able to speak. But Isaac couldn't speak. In fact, he rarely made any sound at all. No doctor had been able to work out why. But if Noah became famous, he would have enough money to find a cure.

* * *

A year rolled by, and one morning, Noah got out of bed early, as he always did to make a video before school. He put on his worn school uniform and went down to the kitchen and set up his iPhone to record. It was, as you might have guessed, a very battered old iPhone. The cracked camera lens meant his videos were a bit blurry. But other than that, it still worked all right. Today he was making Flipping Flapjacks. These gave you so much energy, you would be able to do backflips for a whole hour afterwards.

After he was done recording, he edited and uploaded the video.

"I wonder if I'll get more than three likes this time," he thought to himself.

He spotted a notification in the corner of the page. A new subscriber! Noah clicked on their profile. "Access denied" he read.

"That's strange," he said to himself.

He refreshed the page and clicked on the profile again. He got the same error message as before, "Access denied."

"Who would create an account, only to restrict all access to their profile," he thought. He glanced at the time and realised he needed to go.

He put on his school bag and grabbed a piece of toast. Then he ran out to catch the bus to school.

When he got to the bus stop, his best

friend, Arthur, was there to meet him.

Arthur was also Noah's only friend.

"Hi, Noah," he said.

"Morning, Arthur."

"Are you excited?"

Noah was confused. "Excited about what?"

"Don't you remember? Today is Secret Box Day!" said Arthur eagerly.

"Oh, yes!" Noah gasped. "Of course it is. I forgot all about it!"

CHAPTER TWO

The New Button

A few years ago, the government had introduced a new scheme. It was called 'Red Trip, Blue Trip'. This scheme offered a choice of two school trips to every child in the country at the end of the school year. Each child would choose to go on a red bus or a blue bus, and each bus would travel to a different place. The trips were always really fun. Last year, for example, the red bus at Noah's school went to a film studio tour. The blue bus had gone to a disco bowling alley. The government also provided goodie bags full of sweets and snacks. The sweets weren't as good as Noah's, of course, but they were still pretty great!

The way they chose their trips was mysterious and strange. It was partly why Secret Box Day was so exciting. The teacher would get out a black box. Inside the box were two buttons. One red, one blue. Each child would wait their turn to look inside and press one of the buttons. The box was black so nobody else could see what they chose. This was to avoid them all picking trips just because their friends did. At least, that's what they'd been told.

Today was that day. Noah and Arthur were so excited by the time they arrived at school.

"I can't believe I forgot!" said Noah. "I never forget. I love Secret Box Day."

"Me too," replied Arthur.

Suddenly, somebody walked right into Noah's shoulder. It was Elijah, and it hadn't been an accident.

"Hey, watch where you're going." Elijah

sneered. "This is a two-thousand-pound jacket! My housekeeper will have to dry-clean this now that you've touched it! I only unwrapped it this morning. The video's had nine hundred views already."

"Good for you," said Noah.

"Yeah, it is," said Elijah smugly. "And I recorded it on my new iPhone. The quality's fantastic. Shame your videos are still so blurry."

Elijah's friends laughed in agreement.

"Yeah, well, we aren't all spoilt like you," said Noah under his breath as he walked away.

* * *

It was almost time to choose their trips. All the children in Noah's class sat quickly. They were eager to hear where the buses would be going this year. Once everyone was settled, Ms Prince began to speak.

"Now, children. As you know, today is Secret Box Day. This year, the red bus will be going to the beach and the blue bus will be going to Alton Towers."

Giddy chatter broke out across the classroom.

"Children, settle down, please. I know that's thrilling news, but I want to get this done as swiftly as possible. We've got lots of learning to do today."

The class quieted and waited for Ms Prince to continue.

"Now, as usual, the trips will take place in three weeks. Please form an orderly line and wait your turn to approach the black box. Once you have chosen, the box will print you a bus ticket. Do not lose it! Without it, you cannot board your bus and will have to spend the day doing geography worksheets with Mr Thompson."

As Noah waited his turn, he thought about last year and suddenly remembered the green button. Had he imagined it? Would it be there again?

"Noah, come forward, please and do not take too long," snapped Ms Prince.

Noah walked up to the box and peered inside. There it was again- the green button.

He checked by touching them in case his eyes were playing tricks on him. One red, one blue, and definitely one green. He considered just pressing green to see what would happen.

His hand hovered over it- should he? But he delayed too long.

"Right that's it" shouted Ms Prince. She slammed the box shut.

"You are staying in school instead of going on a trip. I've had enough of everyone taking so long, I'm making an example out of you. Move along.

Noah was devastated.

CHAPTER THREE

Green

Another year passed. Nothing much had changed. Noah's YouTube channel was still as unpopular as ever. Elijah's channel was still as *popular* as ever. Isaac still hadn't learnt to speak.

But today was Secret Box Day again. That got Noah's spirits up. The gold mine had been incredible, and he had missed last year's due to the strict Ms Prince.

As he approached the black box, he knew exactly what he was going to choose. Ms Prince had told them the blue bus was going to a dry ski slope, which was cool. But the red bus was going to a cake factory, which was right up Noah's street. He peered into the box, ready to press the red button. But there it was again. The green button.

Noah hesitated.

"Get on with it, Noah." Ms Prince tutted impatiently. "Or it's Mr Thompson and those geography worksheets."

Should he press it? Or shouldn't he?

He did not want to miss the trips again, so he panicked, closed his eyes and slammed his hand onto the green button! What had he just done? His heart raced. A white ticket appeared from the machine and he took it. It looked the same as everyone else's ticket-with a black QR code on it. He took his ticket and sat down silently in his seat.

Over the next three weeks, Noah couldn't stop thinking about the green button. He didn't want to mention it to his friends. He'd already got the nickname Greeny from two years ago when he talked about it. He didn't dare bring it up again.

What did the button mean? Where would he be going? Did he imagine it? Surely there would be a green bus, wouldn't there?

The night before the big day, Noah didn't sleep a wink. He was too nervous about what the next day would bring. He tossed and turned until the sun came up.

* * *

Noah approached the school gates the next morning. He saw red and blue buses parked in the car park, as expected. There was no green bus. In fact, nothing seemed different at all. He began to panic.

What should he do? He'd thought it would be obvious.

He stood at the gates for ages, until Ms Prince snapped him out of it.

"Hurry up and board your chosen buses, please, children. They are leaving in five minutes, whether you are on them or not!"

As far as Noah could work out, he had no choice but to pick a bus. He chose red. The cake factory trip. He handed his ticket to the driver, who scanned the barcode. The scanner made a horrible buzzing sound. *GUUZZZZZZZZZ.*

"Sorry," said the driver. "This ticket's for another bus. Off you go, now."

Noah left the red bus, feeling worried and even more confused.

"I guess I'll get on the blue bus, then," he said to himself.

He boarded it and handed his ticket to the driver. *GUUZZZZZZZZZ.* The same thing happened.

"You must be on the wrong bus, young man," she said.

"I guess so," said Noah.

He walked away from the blue bus. Panic at the thought of spending the day with Mr Thompson rose in his chest. He was starting to feel quite sick.

But at that moment, something caught his attention. A flash of light bounced off a green bonnet in the distance. There it was. Parked just behind a tree at the end of the road. A small, bright green bus.

"I knew there would be a green bus," Noah whispered as he marched towards it.

The sick feeling left his stomach as quickly as it arrived and was replaced by nothing but excitement.

CHAPTER FOUR

More Than One Bus

As Noah approached, it became clear that the bus was just like the blue and red ones. It was definitely part of the same government scheme. He stepped up cautiously. What was going to happen?

He handed his ticket to the driver, who scanned it. *PING!* It was accepted right away. So fast, it made Noah jump a little.

"Make your way down to seat ten and buckle your seatbelt," said the driver.

Noah was a bit nervous when he noticed he was the only passenger on the bus. But still, he did as he was told.

Surely more passengers would arrive

soon, he thought.

Nobody else came. He could see the other two buses filling up in the distance. Had he made a huge mistake?

"Leaving in one minute!" the driver called.

Noah began to panic again. He didn't like this. He wanted to get off! He went to unbuckle his belt and leave, but the belt was jammed. Locked. He fiddled with the buckle. He tugged and shook. But it was no good. His heart began to pound in his chest.

"Help! Let me off. HELP!" he cried. But the driver said nothing. Instead, she started the engine and drove off.

Noah was very stressed now. He pulled out his phone to call home. But there was no signal at all. He couldn't phone. He couldn't text. He couldn't contact anyone in any way.

"What?! There's always a signal here," he exclaimed. "What's going on?"

But there was nothing to be done. He

was stuck. He had no choice but to see where this bus was taking him. He reassured himself that it was fine. The school wouldn't have sent him on this trip if it wasn't right, would they? Surely nothing bad would happen.

As he calmed down, Noah realised how tired he was. This wasn't too surprising. He had hardly slept for days. He drifted off as the bus turned onto the motorway.

* * *

Noah was woken suddenly by the sound of his heavy belt buckle releasing. *CLUNK!* He rubbed his eyes and peered out the window. He was at the airport. They were parked at the end of a row of other buses, all green. The driver escorted the sleepy Noah off the bus and into a waiting room full of other children.

They all seemed relaxed.

They all seemed like they knew they were supposed to be there.

Noah felt quite uncomfortable. He stood nervously at the edge of the room.

"Hello!" said a bright voice next to him. "I'm Isabelle. What's your name?"

Noah jumped slightly. "Oh! Hi. Hello," he stuttered. "I'm... I'm Noah."

"Hi, Noah," said Isabelle. "What's your YouTube channel about?"

"I'm sorry?" Noah was confused. "How do you know about my—"

"Mine's about sewing and making clothes," she interrupted. "Not very popular, though. I've only got four subscribers, and two of them are my mum! I made this dress. Do you like it?"

This was a lot of information to take in. "Um..." mumbled Noah.

But before Noah could ask any questions, their conversation was cut short.

"Gather round, children," called an air

hostess. "Before we board the plane, I just want to remind you why you are all here."

"Come on," said Isabelle, grabbing Noah and leading him across the room. "I'll look after you. You seem a bit sleepy."

"As your parents have explained to you…" began the hostess.

My Mum didn't explain anything at all, thought Noah.

"…you have all been chosen by the government as creators of exceptional talent. Your YouTube channels are fantastic. You are being offered the chance to teach your skills to some of the people of Malawi. The green button appeared to you because of an algorithm planted on your phones. This was done through your YouTube channels. The button only appeared when your phone was nearby. That's why only you could see it."

"This is so exciting," panted Isabelle, jumping up and down. "Are you excited,

Noah?"

"Um. I guess so," he replied. "I wasn't told about any of this, though."

"Oh well." She shrugged. "You're here now. And like I said, I'll look after you."

"Thanks," said Noah. He liked Isabelle. She was very energetic.

"Now, if you'll all follow me," said the hostess, "we have a plane to board!"

Before he knew it, Noah was in the air on his way to Malawi. What had he got himself into?

CHAPTER FIVE

The Deadline

Noah really enjoyed the flight. The hostess served them the fanciest plane food he had ever seen. Isabelle filled him in on everything he didn't know. She told him everyone on the plane had a different skill to teach. Skills like computing, plumbing, electronics, and building. In return for their efforts, the government would boost their YouTube channels. They would also provide them with new, top-of-range phones to record on once they got home.

But there was a catch.

A deadline.

They had to upload their videos by

midnight on the second day they were in Malawi, or the deal was off. Not only that, but their families would have to pay for the whole trip. It cost nearly twenty thousand pounds! Noah's family did not have that kind of money.

"This is still so confusing," said Noah. "Why didn't anyone explain this to me?"

"Don't worry," said Isabelle. "I'm sure your teacher meant to tell you. Maybe she was busy?"

"She does seem busy. That's probably why she's grumpy all the time," said Noah.

"Listen," said Isabelle, "this is a great opportunity."

"How do you know?" asked Noah.

"A girl called Nora at my school pressed the green button a few years ago. Her channel about carpentry is so famous now. She's even in talks to have her own TV show!"

Noah still felt unsure.

"Look, we're landing now. You're here!

You might as well make the most of it. There's no turning back."

* * *

As soon as they arrived at the Malawian village of Zambu, Isabelle got stuck in. She couldn't wait to pass her skills on to the family she was staying with. She was being looked after by an old woman called Rosie. Rosie was amazing at making clothing from recycled materials. She only had basic equipment too, which made it even more amazing. Isabelle was going to teach her about fashion trends and how to recreate them using new supplies and equipment. She'd brought needles, coloured thread, and even a new pedal-powered sewing machine!

Noah felt very out of place. All the other children seemed to know exactly what they were doing. He wasn't prepared at all. Luckily for him, he was staying with the kindest woman he could ever remember meeting.

Grace was a single mother of six children. She didn't have much, but she shared all she had. She put Noah in his own bedroom and cooked him food with the best ingredients. He was very quiet at dinner. So, once all the children had left the table, Grace patted his hand.

"You seem sad," she said. "Is everything all right?"

"I'm just feeling homesick. I'm not sure I should be here," answered Noah.

"Nonsense. Of course you are supposed to be here," she told him. "Everything happens for a reason. You are here because you are a talented young man with a gift to share."

"How will me making sweets help you?" asked Noah. "Other children are teaching plumbing, computing, and building. What use are my Fizzing Fire-

Chews?"

"Everybody loves sweets. Yes, we need buildings, good plumbing, and computers. But we live for things like sweets. Besides, if you teach me to make sweets, then I can start a business. A sweets business will bring my family the money it desperately needs. I have six mouths to feed and a hole in my roof that needs fixing!"

"I guess you're right," said Noah. "But what if I fail? What if I don't make a video in time? What if my family have to pay for the trip? My brother can't speak. If my parents have to pay for this, they'll never be able to afford a cure for Isaac."

"That's interesting" said Grace, leaning in. "My third son, Kwame... he can't speak either."

"But he spoke at dinnertime," said Noah, confused.

"Indeed, he did," said Grace with a raised eyebrow. "I make a herbal potion that gives him the ability to speak. Now, how about you share your gift with me tomorrow and make your video? In return, I shall teach you how this potion is made."

Now Noah was not only relaxed, he was excited.

"You're on!" he said with a big smile on his face.

CHAPTER SIX

The Herbal Potion

The next day when Grace awoke, Noah had already been up for hours. He was in the kitchen and had a lot going on. He'd laid out ingredients. There were four huge pots boiling on Grace's old stove. All of them had something delicious and sticky inside. He had set up his smashed old iPhone on a rickety tripod.

"Wow. This all looks amazing," said Grace. "The smell is wonderful."

"Thanks, Grace," said Noah brightly. "I've got so much to show you. I can't wait!"

"And you record your videos on this phone?" she asked, pointing at the iPhone.

"That's right. The camera's not the best, but it works," explained Noah.

"How fascinating. I've never used technology like it," said Grace with wide eyes.

Well, there you go, thought Noah to himself. He spent so much time moaning that his phone wasn't the latest model. Grace didn't even have a mobile phone. Perhaps he should be a bit more grateful.

Noah and Grace spent all morning cooking. Noah filmed every bit of it with his camera. He planned to edit and upload it later that evening.

He taught her to make all of his classic sweets, from Fizzing Fire-Chews through to Caramel Cushions. He had to adapt his Tangerine Tongue Toffees a bit, because there were no tangerines for miles. But Noah was very skilled. They may not have had tangerines, but they *did* have mangoes. The invention of Mango Mouth Munchies was a great success!

After Noah taught Grace all he could teach, and filmed all he could film, it was Grace's turn. She spent the afternoon teaching Noah how to make her special herbal potion. It was made from a few simple herbs, a handful of nuts, and some water. That was the easy bit. The tricky bit was *how* you brewed the potion. You had to heat it very slowly to just the right temperature. Then, you also had to stir it exactly seven times every seven minutes until it turned purple.

"I can't thank you enough for this. It's going to change my family's life!" said Noah.

"You are welcome," said Grace. "And anyway, you shared your wonderful gift with me. It is only fair that I share mine with you."

* * *

All seemed to be going very well until later that night.

It was coming up to midnight. The deadline had nearly arrived. Noah had just finished editing his video when he heard a sudden rumble. Then he saw a terrifying flash of lightning through his bedroom window. *KRACKOOOOOOOWWW!*

A storm. And a big one too. It only lasted ten minutes, but it did a lot of damage. Trees had fallen. The river overflowed. Anyone who was caught outside ended up soaking wet and shivering. But worst of all, the village's only power mast was destroyed. There was no electricity and no way of uploading anything to the internet. Midnight was only half an hour away, and not a single child had uploaded a video.

Everyone began to panic.

CHAPTER SEVEN

Only One Bar

There were children running all over the village, trying to work out what to do.

"We have to find a way to upload our stuff," said a tall boy with curly hair. "If my family has to pay for this trip, we'll have nothing left!"

"Don't worry," said Isabelle coolly. "I'm sure we'll find a way."

"How can you be so sure?" asked a small girl with lots of freckles on her nose. "We've only got twenty-six minutes until midnight!"

"Are you going to magic some signal up out of thin air?" asked the curly-haired boy angrily.

"Bit rude… but he might have a point," said Noah, worried.

The noise and worry got louder and louder. Everyone was talking over each other. Suddenly, a man appeared and tried to interrupt them.

"Everybody calm down," he said.

The noise continued.

The man bellowed this time. "EVERYBODY CALM DOWN!"

The children fell silent.

"I can help," continued the man. He was one of the people who'd helped organise when they first arrived, Noah remembered. "There is a power mast a ten minutes' drive away. It's at the top of that big hill over there. My truck is big enough to take you all. If we leave now, we might just make it in time!"

"Well, what are we waiting for? Let's go!" yelled Noah.

So go, they did. They all squeezed

into the back of the beaten truck. They were racing down a bumpy road just three minutes later.

Ten minutes after that, the truck ground to a halt.

"Quick. Get out and get uploading," shouted the man. "It's seven minutes until midnight!"

The children did just as he suggested. They clambered out and got as close to the mast as possible. They opened their laptops and unlocked their phones.

"How much signal have you got?" Noah asked Isabelle.

"Only one bar. You?"

"Same," said Noah nervously.

Noah hit the 'upload' button and watched anxiously as the video uploaded very slowly. At two minutes to midnight, the file finally made it onto Noah's YouTube channel.

He had done it.

He could hear sighs of relief coming from the other children, one by one, as their videos went up successfully. Somehow, they had all managed to make it happen!

"We must go now," said the man.

"What?" exclaimed the curly-haired boy. "Can't we stay for a while to see if we get any new likes or comments?"

"Yeah," agreed the girl with the freckled nose. "I want to see if my subscriber numbers go up."

"You can stay if you want." The man chuckled. "But there is another storm coming in. So, unless you want to be struck by lightning or washed down the hill, you should come with me."

"But we've no signal in the village," said Noah. "How will we know if people like our videos?"

"I guess you'll have to wait until you get to the airport tomorrow," said the man. "There will be a signal there."

Noah and the other children weren't happy about this. But they had no other choice. They trundled back down the hill in the truck. The relief they'd all felt after uploading their videos had been replaced by nerves again.

Did the government think they'd done a good enough job? Had they managed to gain followers? Were they about to get the overnight success they'd all dreamed about?

There would be no answers to any of these questions until they had spent one last, very sleepless night in Zambu.

CHAPTER EIGHT

Subscribers

The journey back to the airport was very quiet. The government had sent a huge green bus that fit all the children to take them to the airport. Nobody said a word to anybody else. Everyone was so anxious. Some children were biting their nails. Others tapped their feet or hummed nervously under their breaths. The only person who didn't seem to be tense was Isabelle.

"Are you excited to find out how your video has done?" she asked Noah, breaking the silence.

"How do you manage to be so positive all the time? Aren't you worried?" he replied.

"What's to worry about? We all did as we were asked, didn't we? We've got nothing to lose. Even if we don't get more subscribers to our channels, we still had an amazing trip, don't you think?"

This was why Noah had grown to like Isabelle so much. She always saw the good in every situation. It was another reminder that he could do to be a bit more grateful at times.

"Yes. Yes, of course. You're right," he said. "I'll try to relax. I'm sure it'll all be fine." Noah didn't completely believe the words he'd just said. But he tried really hard to be positive for the rest of the journey. He plugged in his headphones and listened to some relaxing music. He watched as the Malawian countryside flew past his window.

It was when the bus entered the airport car park that Noah heard the first ping. *PING!* Somebody had just got a notification. Then came another ping. And another. And another.

PING…

PING…

PING, PING, PING, PING, PING!

He looked down at his phone and saw his signal was now at full capacity. Five whole bars. That's when things got a bit crazy. The bus was full of the sound of pinging. Noah's own phone was exploding with likes, comments, and subscriptions. Every video from every child had gone viral!

By the time Noah got on the plane, he'd barely started reading the comments he'd received. There were so many!

The hostess' voice crackled out over the plane's Tannoy. "Hello, everyone. We are about to take off. Please buckle your seatbelts and turn off your mobile phones."

"Aww. But I want to read my comments," moaned Noah.

"Oh, come on," said Isabelle. "They'll still be there when we land. Just relax and enjoy the ride. I think things are going to be a bit mad when we get back."

CHAPTER NINE

Back to School

Isabelle was right, as always. Things were very mad indeed when they landed. As soon as they left the departure lounge, reporters were everywhere. Cameras were clicked. Questions were yelled. The airport staff had to push them out of the way to make sure the children got safely back on their buses.

As Noah's green bus pulled away, he watched out the back window. The reporters were running after him, still taking photos and shouting questions. But behind them, far in the distance, he could see Isabelle waving at him from her own green bus.

He waved back with a sad smile. Noah was going to miss his new friend. He knew they'd stay in touch. But she had looked after him so well the last few days, it felt odd to be without her.

The rest of the journey was quite uneventful. Noah felt lonely all of a sudden. Noah had been surrounded by new people, new places, and exciting experiences for the last three days. But now he was on his own. It was only now that he had a moment to himself that it all hit him. He looked at his phone, which was still churning out notifications every second.

"Am I famous now?" he wondered.

His question was answered as soon as he pulled up to the school gates. Every student was there to greet him. There were banners, and balloons, and noise.

So much noise.

It was a lot to take in. It almost felt like he had become a pop star overnight.

Ms Prince, of all people, pulled him from the bus and gave him a huge hug. "Welcome home, Noah. Well done!"

"Thanks, Ms Prince," said Noah, a little confused. She had never so much as cracked a smile at him. And now this.

The crowd around Noah tightened. Everyone wanted to touch him or ask him about his trip. They all wanted autographs and to know how to make his incredible sweets. Even Elijah wanted a piece of the action.

He pulled Noah towards him. "Awesome stuff, Noah. Awesome. Your channel is so cool. I can't believe I never watched it before. We should collab sometime."

The most popular boy in school had just asked Noah to collaborate with him. This was another world!

Noah spent the next hour telling everyone all about his big adventure. But very soon, he'd had quite enough. All this attention was wonderful, but all he really wanted to do was to go home.

He wanted to see his mum.

He wanted to see Isaac.

CHAPTER TEN

Isaac

The front door clicked shut behind Noah as he entered his house.

"Noah? Honey, is that you?" called his mum.

"Yeah. It's me, I'm back!" Noah shouted down the hallway.

His mum came rushing in. "Noah. My baby! Oh, you must tell me everything. How was your trip? Did you manage to make your video?"

"Wait. You knew about the trip?" asked Noah.

"Of course I did," she replied. "Do you think the school would have sent you off to

Africa without telling me? Honestly, Noah, you are funny. I just wanted it to be a surprise, so I didn't tell you!"

"Well, I wish you had. I was a bit unprepared," said Noah.

"Oh, well. I'm sorry. I'll tell you next time. Now, did you upload your video?"

"Yes. I did," Noah said. "It went viral. There were reporters at the airport. Everyone at school mobbed me when I got back. My channel hit ten thousand subscribers overnight! I think I might be famous now. But that's not even the best part?"

"What could be better than all that?" asked Mum.

"Well, the lady I stayed with showed me something life-changing."

"Life-changing?" asked Mum. "What did she show you?"

"Come with me." And with that, Noah led his mother to the kitchen and set about putting Grace's herbal potion together.

"What are you making?" she asked.

"Just wait and see, Mum. I'll be done soon. I need to concentrate."

So, as Noah carefully finished the potion, his mum watched him in curious silence.

Eventually, after some very careful brewing, the potion was ready.

"Watch this… ISAAC!" Noah called.

Noah's little brother crashed into the room excitedly.

"Hey, little brother. I've made you a special drink," he explained, pouring purple potion into a cup. "Want to try some?"

Isaac nodded. He took the cup, licked his lips, and sipped the potion.

"Well," Noah asked nervously, "how does it taste?"

Isaac looked down at the drink. He pursed his lips.

"Not so good?" Mum guessed from his

lack of excitement.

Noah ignored her and repeated the question. "How does it taste, little brother?"

A silence followed. It felt like ages.

And then, just as Noah was about to lose hope, a big smile appeared across Isaac's face. He looked up at his brother and replied. "It's delicious. Thank you."

Noah's mum nearly fainted in surprise. "What is going on? How did you do that, Noah?"

"It's a speaking potion. I learnt it in Malawi." Noah smiled.

Noah's mum burst into tears. Tears of joy. .

She screamed and yelled and sang.

She danced around the kitchen. She banged spoons against pots. She hugged her sons so hard, their eyes nearly burst out of their heads!

"Well, I think it's safe to say this is the best day ever!" she said breathlessly.

"I think you might be right," agreed Noah.

"Me too," said Isaac.

Printed in Great Britain
by Amazon